The Colors
of Love

Leon del Ciervo

STARbooks Press
Sarasota, Florida

Photography Courtesy of Brown Bag Co., Hollywood, CA, USA
Call 1-800-222-9622 for catalogue

Library of Congress Card Catalogue
No. 91-068364

ISBN No. 1-877978-31-0

Contents

This book was underwritten in part by a grant from
The Florida Literary Foundation.

INDEX
of First Lines to the Poetic Visions

"...d'un poeta
non disprezzate il detto!
Udite! Non conoscete amor?
Amor, divino dono, non lo schernir
del mondo anima e vita e l'Amor!

Umberto Giordano, <u>Andrea Chenier</u>
Improvisso, Act One.

To Fausto

who for many years,
long ago in our native land,
gave me happiness.

My Country

The magical beauty of the royal palm
Harmony of wind and waves
in continuous rhythm over ivory sand.
I want to rest under your shadow
and fall sleep with your murmur of peace.

Persona

Everyday he wears the mask,
mask of strength.
Don't touch it!
So often he wears the mask,
mask of wisdom.
Don't touch it!
He is going in public.
Give him the mask of self-assurance.
Don't touch it!
Masks of mosaic,
masks of straw and air.
Where is the man?
Is there a man?
Off with the masks,
the face is faceless,
the body is smoke.
Shadows inside.
The name is failure.

The Parody of Real Love

The player came out of his own body.
He looked at all his toys.
Some were broken, others yet untouched.
The player was tired of the daily game
but knew he had to play it.
"Take your cross and follow me."
Can anyone realize that toys could be
a cross in disguise?
The player looked at himself,
from outside himself
and patiently gathered the playthings
for next day's performance.

Patpong:
Dante's Inferno Revisited

I had heard of Patpong and I was very curious.
Hell of the City of Angels,
Patpong, the cesspool of the world.

I thought I had seen everything.
I thought I'd done a lot
but I was not prepared
for what I saw in Patpong.

Patpong catered to pleasures,
no matter how distorted.
Money could buy anything.
Children with old age eyes,
prostitutes of all kinds,
men, women, epicenes,
with drugs of every type.

No one who has not seen it
can imagine Patpong,
fascinating, repulsive, perverse,
malodorous and fragrant.

I don't know if it still is.
I'm glad I saw it once
but I would not repeat my visit.
It was a unique experience
never to be had twice
I've been back in the Orient,
I've seen Bangkok again
but Patpong for me is dead.

After my first trip to the Orient.

Our Dark Side

Void that appears full,
meaningless eddies that whirl upon themselves,
black that appears white,
NOTHING, NOTHING, NOTING.

Weakened river running nowhere.
Polluted course of water
that disappears In the infinite sands.
There is no trace of life
left by the sterile stream
that might as well never had been.

Variation on the theme:

Some trickle of water
that wastes itself in the desert.
No one will ever again taste the erstwhile sweet water
or relief his thirst
with its freshness.
And the trickle of water will be tears
swallowed by the silent earth.

Yearning

What is what we want?
Hard to say.
The love we imagine,
the love that gives joy and sadness.
I think I know the red love.
I think I know the blue love.
Like in the flame
one burns and leaves nothing;
the other, for a while, gives life,
and when it is gone
leaves us always with a smile in the soul.

Hope

I am the arid land,
parched, sterile,
wasted.
Gardener of heaven,
preserver of nature,
that is not yet hurt by the boar,
rain on me
and give life for a few minutes,
just a few minutes more,
to the incurable territories of my thirsty soul.

Fulfillment

Who can know another person
when we hardly know ourselves.
To say you know someone
you have first to stop living,
stop being you as an individual
and offer yourself as food and sacrifice
to the hungry god that is your aim.
And that we both have done.

Projections of the Mind Just Before Dawn

To Allan B.: Do Not Be Afraid, Be Yourself

I have been for some time haunted by an absurd situation.
Gusts of images and dust of thoughts have flashed in my
mind pointing to some direction. In a way it was a pregnancy
of the mind and of the feelings. And as all pregnancies
have to come to an end, the moment of birth of whatever
was being created finally came. Here is the creature. I believe
it is meaningful and beautiful, as all things are that come
 spontaneously into the world. And it is yours.

White sands of the arena
under the scorching sun,
cold as ice burning the foundations of life.

The gladiator is naked,
dressed in his crystal armour,
feeling millions of eyes on him,
non existent public,
ghost spectators
of a simplistic difficult ballet.

His steel hangs limp,
confused sword that ignores its power.

Something comes to him.
Shapeless,
Grey.
Perhaps the enemy?

The big fat lady with the diamond ring.
The proper gentleman in the pin-stripe suit.
They offer the gladiator a pair of glasses for his eyes
and a dry martini before dinner.

The naked fighter is no longer naked.
He is in disguise,
clothed in a pair of glasses
and in the inner blanket of the gin.
He feels now strong,
he can fight...the enemy?

The enemy is clad in one thread of silver
or, Is it a cobweb?

No weapons.
He has put the truth on his brow.
"I do not want to fight, gladiator,"
"I want to live."
"I want you the victor, my victor,
the victor of life.'

"As I am, I come to you."
"There will be pale coral
to warm your icy steel,
waves of hot moisture
calling on the hidden fire that lies in your sword."

"Forget the dry martini,
throw the glasses at the big fat lady
and send away the proper gentleman."
"Your sword will be unsheathed,
glorious, throbbing in victory.

" I am not your enemy gladiator.
I am gentle."
"I am your sacrificial lamb,
Agnus Dei qui tollis pecata mundi."
"I will take the sins from you."
"Crucify me on the tree of your life,
maybe you will feel strong enough
and you will transfix me with your holy lance."

"Life has two bloods.
One is red.
The other is white.
I want your white blood in my red blood."

And when the sacrifice is over
you will find that the world exists.
The arena will not be bleak,
powdered bones under the sun.

There will be water,
and greenery,
and the gladiator,
gladiator no more,
will be in peace,
dressed in courage,
wiser,
and then the true meaning of the sacred word
will be known to him.

Friendship-love,
unsullied,
fulfilled in itself
because you will have found a friend.

December, dawn of the fourteenth day. Silence and
serenity reign outside and in me. May they reach you,
bringing a smile to your lips while you sleep.

For A.B. with true affection.

Wilson:
Wave in the Water

When we first met the water scared him.
I taught him how to swim.
The last time I saw him he was a pool lifeguard.

Wilson was short,
well-proportioned and muscular
and from my point of view
nothing to rave about.
He had girlfriends galore.
With one of them he married.
His only talk was "women."

Much to my great surprise
his were the first advances.
When we got horizontal
his long pentup repressions
exploded all at once.
It was easy to see
that he was all anxiety and eagerness,
making up for his ignorance.

Even after his marriage
he continued to see me.
His techniques improved much
and he learned to perform
maybe better than swimming.

One day he disappeared.
He stopped coming to school
and I never heard from him.
He left with me a good memory.
I gave him self-assurance.

Tomás:
Cosmic Perspectives

Tomás,
Dominican mulatto,
point of convergence
of the best of two races.
Emeralds in your eyes,
long and languid eyelashes,
skin tanned from the inside
by the sun of your genes,
well defined sensuous lips
that seemed always inviting.

Tomás,
champion of champions
in the jousting of love.
Nine and two and a half inches
of pleasure giving muscle.
Difficult to surpass

Tomás who loved to give.
Tomás who loved to take.
When the moment approached
Tomas who cried: "Give me your all negrito," *
while he gave me his all.

Magnificent finale.
Spastic hugs and tremors
and incoherent babbling
on the part of the two.
Then we exploded in unison.
It was always the same
in perfect timing,
a tremendous orgasm
of galactic proportions.

* *"Negrito", "Negrita" literally meaning little black one,*
  male and female respectively , and "Negro," "Negra" were
  terms of endearment frequently used by lovers.

Mark of the Beast

1

I have not lived that long but I have lived too much.
I have grown very tired.
The curse of living fast,
the sign of the Antichrist,
666,
on my forehead.
It burns deep, it hurts.
Only the tears that flow from blind eyes
can bring relief to that pain.

2

We who live figuratively at night,
we who our numbers are legion,
vampires eternally young
no matter how old we are,
always free,
who couple without issue.
We pay a heavy price.

They no longer hunt us.
Today it is just "another life-style."
They've come to realize
that we do not do harm,
that we can be as honorable
as any next door guy.

They never came to think
that the hunt and the stigma
never accomplished anything,
that only exacerbated
the basic promiscuity
that hides in every man,
maybe not in the woman
but for sure in the man,
whether straight or gay.We are no longer monsters,
but for the lower minds
the curse of the Undead,
the number of the Beast,
are still upon us.

> *Thinking of John, Cardinal O'Connor,*
> *Archbishop of New York.*

Yussuf, Mustafa and Mohamed:

The Colorful Side of Love Making
(or How I Discovered the Long Lost Obelisk of Aswan)

Aswan, southernmost city of Egypt.
Elephantine, the island
where the ram-headed Khnum
makes the Nile flow
from deep caverns beneath,
today, a few native villages
and the Aswan Oberoi.

I had met John in Cairo.
John was a tour guide,
intelligent, well liked.
Most important of all,
member in good standing
of our vast brotherhood.
Of course we became friends,
but nothing more than friends.
John and I were to meet
at the Aswan Oberoi.
He was going with some tourists
and I would be staying there.

I arrived in my room
wanting to take a shower
and have a little rest.
I gave John a phone call.

Marvel of gay efficiency!
Few minutes had elapsed
when someone tapped my door.
With a towel around me
I went to answer the call.
"Good afternoon Sir.
Mr. John said to me
that you'd be pleased with me.
I am a waiter here and my name is Yussuf."

Yussuf was very young,
in his very early twenties.
Tall, dark, slender, handsome,
waves of silky black hair,
the misty eyes of a doe
and a caressing voice.

Needless to say John was right.
Barely an hour arrived,
I was taking a shower
with a beautiful boy
that for sure knew to please.
Interesting beginning!

Later, before nightfall,
Mustafa came to me.
,He was a little older.
More mature.
Stronger frame.
Also handsome and tall.

Mustafa had a job,
a very important job in the Aswan Oberoi.
John had told him about me,
that I was a professor and I enjoyed Archaeology.
He then offered to take me, later that véry night
to see the native villages and the temple of Khnum.

Under the moon we started.
He showed me the villages and what's left of the temple.
Then, in a most courteous gesture
he offered to me his home.

It was a two floor house,
built of adobe and wood,
with a terrace
that overlooked the river.

Those Egyptians work fast.
Without much loss of words,
he wanted to have sex.
An old woman, his servant,
brought out a woven mat.
In a matter of seconds
our clothes had been shed,
my pants, his galabeya,
his turban and my shirt.

Under the stars we made love
and with passion we rode
along the best of roads.
The woman brought mint tea
without the least attention
to our two naked bodies
and their panting gymnastics,

Then came a new arrival,
very tall, very thin.
He too was very handsome.
"This is my friend Mohamed
-said Mustafa-
and he wants to have sex."

I was a little tired,
but...How could I refuse?
A menage a trois in Egypt...

With the speed of lightning
Mohamed stood naked
and How can I decribe
the sight that hit my eyes?
Begging Puccini's pardon
I paraphrased Des Grieux:
"Cossa non vidi mai simile a questa!

I had made a discovery.
Right in front of my eyes
was Aswan's greatest obelisk,
twin brother to Paris',
to Cleopatra's Needle and to Rome's.
The long lost obelisk
believed lost at the sea.

While I feasted my vision
the obelisk came to life,
all by itself,
defying gravity,
immense in all its glory,
throbbing to reach its size.

And what a night that was!
There is no place like Egypt
where pleasure flows so freely,
full of humor,
among beautiful men.

Mohamed performed well;
a virtuoso performance,
a man who knows his instrument
and plays to the sublime.
Mustafa, Mohamed and me,
three live serpents
coiling around each other.
And during the whole ritual
the old woman, unfrazzled,
kept bringing us mint tea.

It was very late
when we finished exhausted.
No question walking back.
My two friendly mates offered to find me a boat.

We walked down to the beach
where some young men played baseball.
We joined them for a while,
stretching our muscles
somewhat sore and achy
by the violent lovemaking.

Finally the boat came.
I was rowed to the mainland
where I took the all-night ferry
to the Aswan Oberoi
but not before agreeing
to have another meeting the next day.

The meeting did take place
next night.
We sailed in Mustafa's felucca,
with the majestic rocks
serving as a backdrop
and the breeze of the river
cooling our boiling blood.
The menage a trois of Egypt
reunited again.

The strange things
never end
in that marvelous land.
Mustafa brought a man,
a man in his mid forties
to take care of the boat
while we rolled in our pleasure.
The poor soul could not take it.
Our moans, grunts and groans
excited him so much
that he took in his hand
the tool of his obsession
and not having a place in our tableau vivant,
masturbated with fury
pouring his life on us.

Mahmoud:
Young Black Sun of Egypt

The strong "rrs" came tumbling from your mouth,
heavily accented English by your Arab speech.
We sat by the river and the breeze of the Nile
softly touched our faces.
Nut arched over us, blue-black and protective,
a thousand chips of light winking at our love.

"I am angry" you said,
"angry because you leave me."
In your Nubian black-blue face,
face of a youthful god,
two diamond drops appeared
that I wiped with a kiss.

I could never forget when we first met.
Hassan, the big Hassan,
the patron of the "Wisky,"
the man who employed you,
confident of his size,
with discretion at first,
more aggressively later,
wanted "to be at my service"
that night in the felucca.
But our eyes had met
and we had shared a cup,
and I refused Hassan

You came for me that night,
contrast of black and white
in your white galabeya.
Something told me to trust you
and I followed you blindly into alleyways and warrens
of the poor Nubian section.

Your house was a mud hut.
No lights except an oil lamp.
The floor was beaten earth.
But it became a palace.

There was light in your eyes
when you looked into me.
I lost my way in it.
Everything was light and,
everything was bright.

Your dark arms, strong and young
encircled all my being.
I melted in those arms.
My heat encouraged yours,
the flowers in your heart
opening in caresses.

In your primitive bed
we became one.
You gave yourself to me,
I gave myself to you
in perfect conjugation.
Lassitude and good feeling.

Suddenly you jumped.
You went to kill a scorpion
that had come near the bed.
I sat naked,
enjoying every ripple,
savoring every curve
of your body of perfection.
Naked in turn you stood,
awkward and very serious.
Probably some responses
learned from other young sailors
or maybe from Hassan.
Maybe the black scorpion that suddenly interfered.
You had to be like the others
or at least you thought so.

"Now you give me two hundred dollars."
I could not help myself,
and I broke out in laughter.
You looked simply so stupid,
not knowing what to say.

With your head in my hands,
your head of Nubian prince,
I caressed and soothed you.
Tenderly I kissed your mouth.
You clinged to me with feeling
and love came to us again.
My lover and my friend.

After that night we were always together,
and when I met your family
there was no need for words.
Fragmented conversation while we sipped the mint tea,
hand gestures did the rest.
Soon Luxor was aware that we were very close
and I was proud of it,
with my blue galabeya, walking right next to you

Then our last night came,
and how could I forget it!
In the warrens and alleys of the poor Nubian section,
your family and your friends,
to say farewell to me
spread out a great banquet.
And we were holding hands.

The walk back to the ship
that would cut us apart.

Your anger,
my sadness,
the ominous open question,
When, if ever, together again?
Can we feel love so fully
that only just few days
seem long as a lifetime?

Farewell Mahmoud of Luxor. Farewell my Nubian God
I intend to return
but if that were not possible
my heart will keep an altar
with your image enshrined.
Inshallah!

Luxor -Second trip to Egypt.

Years later

So many years have passed.
I could never go back
but I have kept my promise.
Deep in my soul your image
receive my daily thoughts.

We kept in touch for some time.
You sent beautiful letters,
envelopes full of roses,
scented petals that spoke of your love,
letters dictated to the public scribe
because you could not write.

More and more dimming health
brought into me the knowledge
that I would never see you
and walk with you
by the Nile;
that the passion so gentle
that we had once experienced
would never be repeated.
But you will be with me,
young black-blue beauty
in memories
that cannot be erased.

Farewell forever my young lover,
May life give you all the goodness
that you rightly deserve!
Allahu Akbar!

Matt: Perfect Beauty

When I looked at the stars
I thought of them as silver nails
decorating the ebony board of heaven.

Then I met you.
The stars were not up high
but on your face,
no longer silver nails.
The stars were lakes,
deep and disturbing,
peaceful and blue. Your eyes.

Pausa en español

L U I S
Juventud vacilante, que
quiere y no se atreve.

1

Pausa en español:

Estrella que se muere
no puede darte luz.
No se la pidas.
Manantial que se seca
no puede darte agua.
No se la pidas.

Partiendo de un punto
dos vidas divergen buscando infinitos diferentes.
Una quiere la calma,
el calor del descanso,
punto final de afanes,
de máscaras,
de imposibles.
La otra, muy joven,
vibra y siente
y quiere, sin poder precisar su deseo,
alzando los brazos para alcanzar el sol
y coger las estrellas.

Mi vida ya no es nada
mientras la tuya empieza.
Abismo gigantesco se tiende entre los dos,
sin que pueda haber puente
que cubra esa distancia.
Solo alas de fénix
o de Pegaso la pueden superar.
Pero el fénix acaba de quemarse en suicidio ritual
y en cuanto a Pegaso, tú no sabes montar a caballo!

Caballero brillante
de los ojos profundos
con tu armadura verde
envuelta en primavera

Te pierdes en la selva
de tus propias preguntas,
te enredas en angustias extrañas
dc paisajes a medias;
querer y no querer,
sentimientos ambiguos
en torrente sin fin.

No te acerques al roble
de ramas retorcidas
y follaje coposo de cambiante color.
El roble que no es roble y te ofrece su fronda.
Te perderás en ella en un calmo descanso.
Solo merece ese descanso quien no lo teme.

Cuídate del arroyo.
Observa que su curso va corriendo al revés.
No bebas de su agua.
Es veneno potente que mata o vivifica,
amargo al que no ama
dulce al que sabe amar.

No hables a la serpiente
de ojos de oro y lengua de seda,
La serpiente es muy sabia,
por vieja y por serpiente.
Si te miran sus ojos o te toca su lengua
ya no seras de ti.
Los anillos del monstruo envolveran tu ser.
Tocarás el infierno,
veras el paraíso,
escalofrio de extasis,
en labios ansiosos del beso final
y ojos cerrados que verán sin mirar.

Caballero brillante
de los ojos profundos,
abandona la selva.
Vuelve tus pobres pasos
hasta tu mismo fondo.

Allí, mira y pregunta,
allí, busca el amor.
Allí que la lluvia te bañe,
que el viento te refresque
y te acaricie el sol.
Que los lirios florezcan desde tu corazón!

Angelo:
Bright Roman Candle

That year I went to Europe
on a musical trip.
At its end, Rome,
for a scholarly meeting.

Angelo was made of music,
melody, harmony and rhythm
were all around his body.
Angelo was a statue
powerful and muscular.
Former soccer player and security guard,
his dark eyes contrasted with his golden skin
and his hair of burnt gold.
"Rubinato" he told me,
exploding into laughter.
Angelo drove the tour bus
and he would be with us
for the length of the trip.

The tour ended in Zurich.
Angelo said to me
"I'm driving back to Italy,
Why don't you ride with me
maybe all the way to Rome?"

The suggestion was excellent.
I would save the train fare.
We had become friends.
I could ride in comfort and with company,
through the Alps,
viewing the Swiss countryside.

As it turned out
Angelo had some tourists to pick up in Milan.
We would spend the night
in a village, not too far from the city
with a quaint little inn, "Albergo di due Leoni."

I invited him to dinner.
After, we went to sleep.
"I always sleep naked," said Angelo to me,
"Do you mind?
Of course I did not mind
although I realized that that night,
sleep would not come easy.

I woke up very early.
I looked to Angelo's bed.
He rested on his back,
one arm bent overhead
with his pillar of fire
proudly standing,
hardened in all its glory.

Occasionally, in his sleep,
he stroked it very gently.

Gioconda's Barnaba sprang in my mind
O monumento!
I lost all my control.
my will power snapped.
In silence I rose from my bed.
In silence I went to his.
My face came down
and my mouth took the place
of his caressing hand.

I did my best.
My best was very good.
Suddenly I realized
Angelo was awake,
but he did not stop me.
His hand caressed my head
as I caressed the center of his feeling.
His body arched,
muscles contracted.
His hands held my head.
And the springs of his fountain
spurted into me
his vital bitter-sweet juices of love

Not a word after that.
In turns we took a shower,
got dressed and went out.
He drove me to Milan,
to the railroad station.
We kissed in the cheek the way old friends do,
as if nothing had happened.
But it had happened, Angelo,
it did take place mio caro,
ragazzo romano, bello come l'alba
gentile e soave come l'aria fresca.

Johnny:
Black Hole of Prejudice

I met him through a "frater"
that taught another subject in the College.
Johnny, young Italian-American who loved singing
and idolized Pavarotti.

The frater had alerted me to Johnny's problem.
He only spoke about women
and of his love affairs,
while his eyes furtively ran to men.

" I like you very much and I respect you a lot,"
"You are the best in the school."
" If I can tell you a secret, sometimes I go with men,
men who are special. I know about your tastes,
and I would love to have you."
 "One thing I must make clear.
I will be the active partner.
Io sono sempre il maschio."
I smiled to myself.

A few days later we got together.
He started his routine.
In just about...five minutes?
He had forgotten it,
no more playing the fable
of the man-man in sex with the man-woman.
As someone who's starving
he gobbled every movement
and devoured each caress,
giving and taking freely.

We went on for some time.
He never admitted his real self in love matters
and he went with his tales of women and their conquest.
One day Johnny got married.
He got fat.
The shine left his eyes
and he lost his smile.

The Dark Maze:
Times Square

Nameless men that moved aimlessly.
All sizes and races
and all colors and hues.

Bodies for sale
for a handful of dollars.
Dignity washed away
in the anonymity of basic instincts.

Not all were nameless.
There were a few I knew.
"I'm pretty:" Jerome.
He certainly was Eddie Murphy's twin brother.
Huge Sam who could hardly speak
but mastered to perfection
all the tricks of the flesh.
Clean and scented Greg
and Eddie, the "innocent preppie."
But most of all, Al Jr. the indisputable king.

They told me they were dangerous.
I never had a problem,
none of them ever harmed me
although some were jailbirds.

Raw pleasure mixed with pity
and if it had been good,
an additional tip,
given in the shadows
of my innermost sub-cellar.

Juan:
The Star That Imploded

1

You are springtime,
fresh water that killed my desert,
sweet breeze calming the fever
of crowded loneliness.

When you came
the flow of time was reversed
and all my pasts became present,
the present that would build our past.

I sat on a rock by the road
looking at life,
without living it,
rows of cardboard dummies
entertaining me briefly.

You alone are alive.
Your touch is hard and tender.
Your lips have the two flames,
bier and cradle of my eternal Phoenix.

The cross of my life was incomplete,
truncated in one arm.
You made it whole and glorious
and from your eyes
sprang the missing limb.

Winter cannot come
no matter how near me.
Your sun has made two One.
The name of One is Love.

2

In the dark of night, seeing the end coming, haunted by
misty old legends and memories.

Parsifal,
young knight of the forest,
Where is your Question?
Your trees turn brown, turn dead,
the Fisher King is dying,
Were you who made the wound?
No. Your Quest was meant to heal.
But the trees turn brown
and the soil dies of thirst.

Young knight of the white armor,
Where is your Question?
In the hall of the castle
the Fisher King is dying.
The procession passed by you.
You have the Lance,
you could have had the Grail

Your lips are mute
young knight of the burnt hopes.
You know not how to ask,
while the wound grows inward
and the rivers go dry.

The Fisher King is dying
the death that does not kill.
Young knight of flaming mind,
words you have,
not the Word.
Why can't you find it Parsifal?
Where is the Word, young knight?

Look in yourself young man
and Parsifal, remember!
You have the Lance that wounds to heal
but not the Word that goes with it.
Your lips are mute my Parsifal.
Where is your Question, Lord,
that you forget to ask?

Gilberto:
Syrius, The Brightest Star, Perfection

1

I moved aimlessly alone.
Sometimes I danced with robots of flesh
that seemed warm
but left on my skin
the mark of cold, rusted metal.

One, two, three, a hundred more,
it was very unimportant.
The same ritual, empty and drafty,
repeated over and over again,
the kiss with open eyes,
bodies intertwined,
impatient to score.

Two explosions that burst one after another,
provoked each by the other,
close in physical ambit,
total strangers really,
light years apart in their microcosms,
leaving two dirty bodies.
Et Nihil.

The wise man bows to reality
and the years create the crust of the cynical crab,
that forgets the truths of myth.
Pandora's box and hope,
Turandot's first enigma: Speranza.

Suddenly a tree grows
and a miracle happens.
Youth looks with fire arrows,
fire that melts the crust.
The crab finds his heart.
The myth is real. It lives.
You made it possible,
you gave it your name.

2

I have walked in darkness a long time.
The stars were forgotten
and the light of my life was no more.

In the long roads of my years,
sometimes during storms
the livid glare of lightning
illumined my yearnings
and sometimes roaring fires
consumed with vivid red the rags of my decency.

But I craved for the light
and I longed for the stars.

Coming to me at my end,
shadow of my self no more
one day and by surprise,
in the midst of the ruins of what I was
my soul found you.

And you were not brief lightning
nor were you red fire.
Knowing it would he an instant,
but an instant of glory
I surrendered to you all of my inner self
and I gave you my soul,
reborn and pure
by the touch of your life

3

To put in words the diverse thoughts,
the variety of feelings
that are centered around you
I cannot.
Castration of the mind
dream I don't dare to dream,
perfection of repressions,
Curse of the fear to lose you

4

Tonight I feel lonely.
It is a loneliness that not for expected
is less cruel or painful.

You know it.
My life had been a whirlwind
with all kinds of entanglements
with persons of all types.
I had known the cheap love
and I have felt the love that ennobles.

I thought my years were finished
when you came.
Knowing you surprised a spirit
that could not know surprises anymore.
If I had known you earlier...!

I realized the impossible
but gave myself to it,
in a total new way,
a way I had forgotten.

What are we? What have we been?
You have been son and brother,
you have been friend and lover
to the best of myself.
You made me be of silver
and you dressed me with life.

Tonight, in isolation,
with your image around me,
in the realization of the end,
not of the love,
not of the understanding
but of the frequent contact
with its shared laughter of the interrupted French
and of the constant present of my beloved Min,
I will lie on your bed
with my head on your pillow,
in vain search for your warmth,
thinking of what you gave me.

I have lost many things
but I will never lose you
Over distance and time my soul will be in your heart,
and your image and essence
conquering time and distance
will stay always with me.

Francisco:
Dark of the Moon
Cruel Selfishness

Why do you haunt me Hoffmann?
You lover of music,
you lover of beauty,
who chased love after love
and remained in the end
with only your own company,
with a heart that is dry,
a heart that knows no moisture
except your bitter blood.

In pursuit of love you have grown old,
and what are you today, dear Hoffmann,
if not "the grandfather" that a youth
is taking to a discotheque?

Shame, shame and three times shame.
Resign yourself old Hoffmann.
For you there is no love
except perhaps in music
and your Egyptian gods.

Are you pedantic, Hoffmann?
Why do you have to shine
blinding the youthful eyes
that know nothing but surface.

All your life you have dreamt
but your dreams have turned flesh,
a flash of sensuous tremor
that exhausts in itself.

No, my pitiful Herr Hoffmann.
Your Olympias, Giuliettas and Antonias
were evanescent ghosts
that melted to your touch.

One made you ridiculous,
the second burned your soul
and the last made you cry.

No love for you, Herr Hoffmann.
Go back to your mirage
and return to your shadows.
Never leave them, poor soul!

After all, with Macbeth you'll agree
that life is nothing but an idiot's tale
and that you, mein lieber Hoffmann
are the poor player"
strutting and pretending
on an empty stage,
whose boards are drenched
with the blood of your soul.

And for you my dear Hoffmann
the pilgrims will not chant
on their way back from Rome.
They will not bring the staff
of the Head of the Church
miraculously green and reflowering white.

You are not Tanhauser, Hoffmann.
No Elizabeth for you.
Finish your life without love.
Plunge yourself in the dark.

*Written with blood in Salamanca. It could have been written in any other
city that we visited. I am sure that you are not familiar with Jacques Offenbach's
"Tales of Hoffmann." It was something I wanted you to see in the Met's present
season. Neither, I am sure, are you familiar with Macbeth or Wagner's
Tanhauser. The day you know them you will understand the references. Mean-
while , let me tell you that you have been for me a mixture of the three heroines
in Offenbach's opera. You made me look ridiculous, you burned my heart and
you also made me cry.*

In Retrospect. Offenbach Again.

Kleinzach, the old clown jester
of sharp mind, of the court of Eisenach.
Ungainly and deformed,
How old are you Kleinzach?
Neither Hoffman nor Offenbach
mention your age Kleinzach.

You forgot yourself clown jester
when one day Youth caressed you.
You became pretentious,
you became ridiculous.

You wanted love Kleinzach.
You mistook the careless caress of the youth
for an impossible desire.
Burn yourself clown jester,
follow your "love", buffoon
all the way down the road.

Something is waiting there
which is not the caress.
When you arrive in the chamber
what you will find Kleinzach,
is a room full of mirrors
reflecting how you are.

After returning from Spain.

THINKING OF YOUNG LOVERS

Ganymedes

Ganymedes wears faded jeans.
He has long hair.
The eagle perched on his rock
has one broken wing.
He cannot anymore swoop down
to abduct Ganymedes.
The eagle cannot take the youth with him
to Olympus.
The eagle smiles sitting on his rock.
He has sworn to love what Ganymedes loves.
Because the eagle has a broken wing
and knows he will fly no more.

Memories of Young Lovers

I have never been hungry
but now I hunger for your soul.
The old vampire is toothless
but his mind still remembers
the sensation of the sharp fangs
biting the source of life.

HUSSEIN:
Sudden Shining Comet

(The Colors of Love)

The Encounter (Petra)

Son that gives me strength.
Brother that gives me help.
Friend that carries my burden.
Lover that gives me LIFE.
They all came on horseback.
I saw your "ugly" face.
The brightness of that face
shining into my heart
took me to realize
I was no longer mine,
that I belonged to you,
from that moment forever.

THE COLOR IS GOLD

The Realization (Aqaba)

Who are you beloved?
Where do you come from, loved one?
What is your secret name?
The name that gives the power,
the name that makes complete,
drop it into my heart.
I found your name beloved,
when I entered your soul.
And now I have the power
and now I am complete.
I know your name habibi.
Your secret name is love.

THE COLOR IS BRIGHT SILVER

The Two Made One (Amman)

I drank the sweetness of my beloved
in his most noble tears.
He has given me life when I tasted his blood,
for his blood is the LIFE.
You are in my heart now
and the warmth of your body
and the crush of your arms
that held me tight to you
in the thickness of our awakening
fused our two selves in ONE.

THE COLOR IS DEEP BLUE

MEMORIES

(After speaking long distance
with my "ugly face" in Jordan)

Life was dark when I met you,
and all my futures were in the past.
My soil was unproductive,
swept by the winds of nothing.
I thought there was no hope
and I missed love so much!
How could I expect beauty?
How could I expect care
when I could give so little?

I don't know how it happened.
I don't know how I loved you,
but before I could think
there you were in my heart.

My body and soul ached for you
and I became your own,
no longer mine but yours,
without any other purpose
than giving you my love

You responded to me
with a warmth and a passion
that I could not believe,
and for just a brief period,
you gave me paradise.

AmFAR American Foundation for AIDS Research

5900 Wilshire Boulevard • Los Angeles, California 90036-5032

Some day -- very soon I hope -- you and I will have tremendous reason to feel proud. That day, when we are able to announce that a vaccine against AIDS has been found, you'll know you played a part in winning a milestone victory for all humankind.

I write today to thank you for your recent renewal contribution, extending your support for AmFAR for the next calendar year.

Loyal and generous support like yours permits us to continue our massive efforts to end the AIDS epidemic through research and education.

The research grants selected by our leading scientific experts for funding ... our innovative Community-Based Clinical Trials program ... our educational projects to help prevent the spread of AIDS ... and our efforts to combat discrimination against people with AIDS ... none of these would be possible without caring contributors like you.

Thanks to you, we are making important progress in the fight against AIDS. (AIDS research has even had the additional benefit of helping to understand and combat other major diseases which have long eluded medical researchers.)

That means your dollars have gone a very long way -- so, once again, I thank you.

Sincerely,

Dr. Joel D. Weisman
Chairman

JW:rn

"...New book about a rock star's secret young lover is deliciously satisfying..."

NEW and RECOMMENDED
from STARbooks Press:
"THE KID: The Confessions of a
Rock Star's Secret Young Lover."
Fiction By JOHN PATRICK
With Joe Leslie
ISBN 1-877978-27-2 $9.95 U.S.

The Kid

The Confessions of a Rock Star's
Secret Young Lover

A Shocking Love Story by
JOHN PATRICK

By the final page of "The Kid," we know
for certain that we are the only ones in
whom the winsome young hero William
has ever confided. We alone have been
invited to understand his unusual, highly
erotic, often touching tale.

In this fast-paced journey that we
typically expect from the author John
Patrick, we are never distant from
William as he struggles to make a
meaningful narrative of his life for
himself, becoming profoundly observant,
often poetic, often wise beyond his years.

We find his sole method of connection
with those around him is through sex. For
the men of his acquaintance, William
embodies the best of sex, the sex they
crave and so seldom find. We picture
William as being a boy so beautiful, so
intuitively sexy that he elicits the reader's
trust and identification, though he is too
intelligent to ever ask for it.

The book becomes deliciously satisfying,
page by page, as we are plunged into
William's dreamworld come true, a world
of Hollywood glamour, wealth, and
occasional

loneliness, the world of his older
lover, former teen idol Joe Skinner,
who is not only sexually confused but
a handsome hunk as well.

Yet we sense, as only those who have
experienced the realities, even the
cruelties of life, can sense it, this
paradise on earth William has found
cannot last.

In the end, we also know there is
something wonderful about this tale,
but what does it all mean? And
William wisely leaves that to the
reader's imagination.

STARbooks Press titles are sold at
fine booksellers throughout the world
and distributed by Inland Book Co.,
Golden-Lee, Turnaround/London and
Stilone-PTY, Ltd., Australia.